Educating Children on Divorce

ISBN 978-1-0980-5094-8 (paperback)
ISBN 978-1-0980-5095-5 (hardcover)
ISBN 978-1-0980-5096-2 (digital)

Christian Faith Publishing, Inc.
832 Park Avenue
Meadville, PA 16335
www.christianfaithpublishing.com

Artwork: Dr. Deborah Hollimon

Printed in the United States of America

Educating Children on Divorce

Dr. Deborah Hollimon

Artwork: Dr. Deborah Hollimon

Hello, everybody! We have a very happy family. There is Daddy, Mommy, brother, Skip, and myself. I'm the sister.

Our family would go on various vacations. We all looked forward to spending time together. We could not wait to plan the next vacation.

Mommy and I would enjoy singing together. Mommy did not know I could sing so well.

Daddy and my brother would play basketball. It was fun to see how many baskets they could each make.

Mommy and I would have fun bike riding together. I loved the time I spent with Mommy.

Daddy and my brother would get their needed exercise by bowling together. They each wanted to see who could knock down the most pins.

Our family enjoyed playing card and board games together.

Our family enjoyed having barbeques. My brother and I enjoyed the hamburgers that Daddy would grill.

Our family would go out to watch movies together. We enjoy watching comedies, adventure, and family movies.

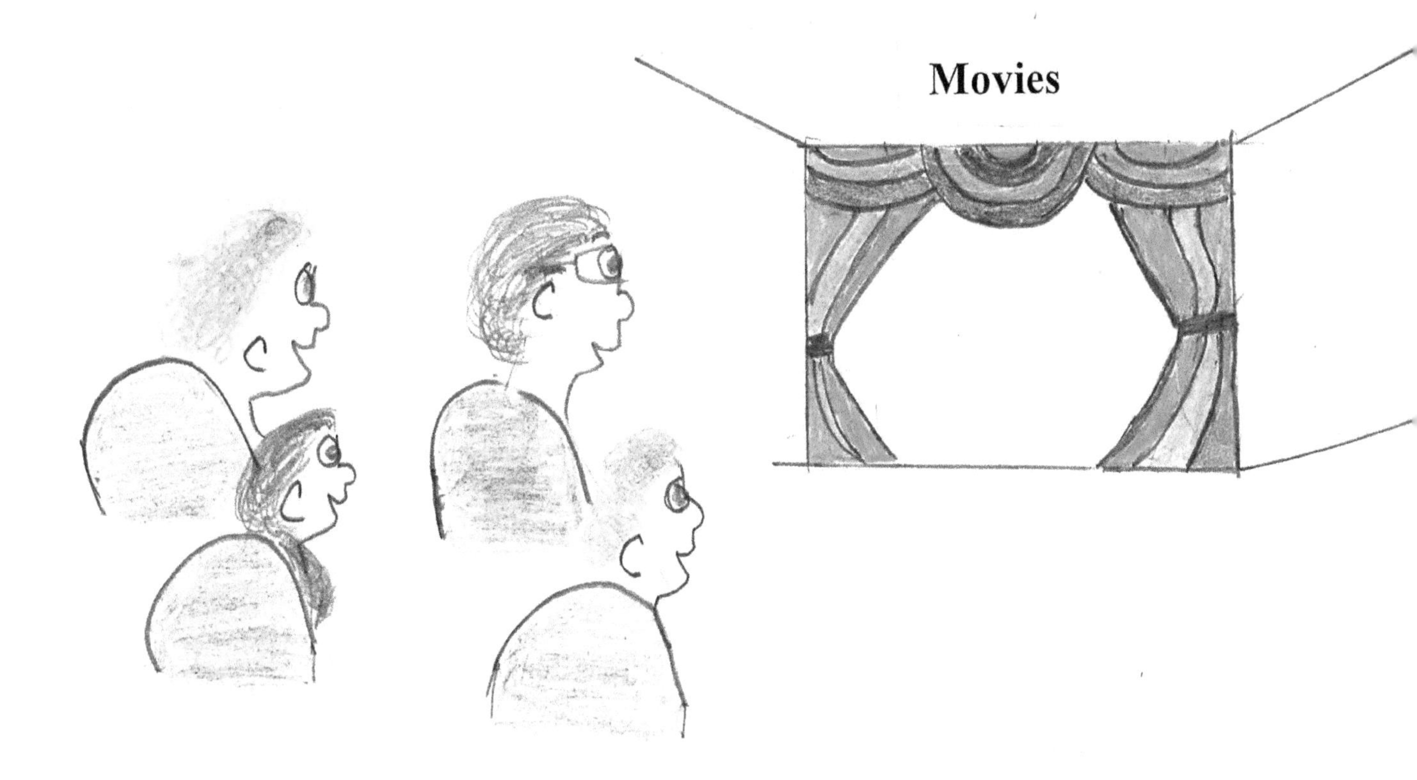
Movies

Then one day Daddy and Mommy came to us and told us they were getting a divorce.

"What is a divorce?" my brother and I asked.

Daddy said, "It is when Daddy and Mommy decided that they are unhappy living together for many reasons. They no longer are married and live apart from each other."

When I found out that our parents were divorcing, I began acting out. I would cry a lot, ate less, and started wetting my bed. I told my mother that my brother was picking on me and called me names for no reason. I told my mother this made me very sad that my brother was acting this way.

Soon after this my brother began yelling and cursing at our parents, especially our mother. My brother began getting bad grades and skipping school. Our parents had to go to the principal to see what could be done. The principal was not aware that our parents were divorcing. The principal suggested that our parents get counseling.

Even our dog, Spot, began getting hyper, barking a lot and had accidents on the floor.

The parents talked to the counselor. She suggested a contract for all of us to sign. The contract showed what our parents agreed upon. Our parents wrote the contract with the help of the counselor.

Our parents wanted us to know that no matter what, we would always be loved. That even though they may disagree they too would respect each other throughout the divorce.

Daddy and Mommy wanted us to know that we did nothing wrong and were not the reason for them divorcing.

Mommy and Daddy wrote a contract for everyone to sign. They put the contract on their refrigerator door at their place so all would be reminded what we agreed upon.

Contract.

My brother and I were very happy that our parents made a contract that everyone signed. We too kept the contract at our bedside. It made us feel happy and safe that our parents would always love us!

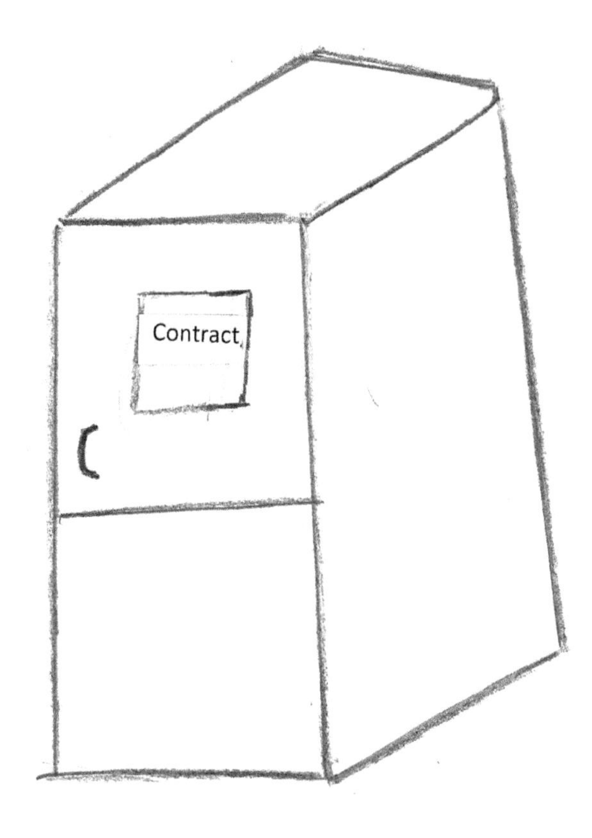
Contract

Family Contract

Date:______________

Daddy_______________(Name) and Mommy_______________ (Name) will always respect each other and love our children.

(Name of each child)

1.______________________

2.______________________

3.______________________

4.______________________

We will be that example of what a loving family should be no matter where we are.

That we will be open and be here for our children whenever then need to speak to us.

This contract will be put on each of our refrigerator door to always remind us that we are family!

And if we do forget at times, we will remind each other what we agreed to.